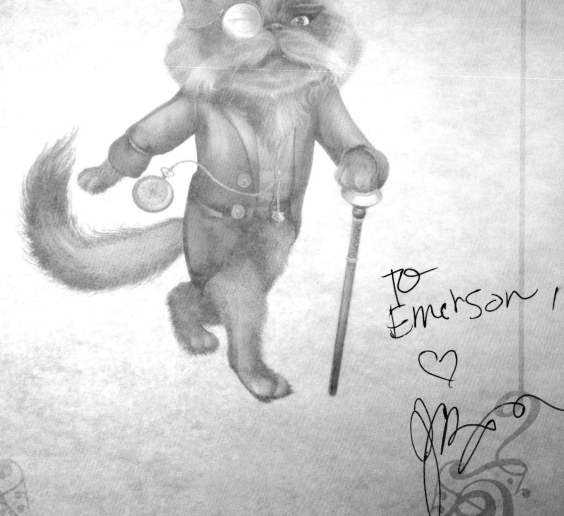

To Emerson!

♡

*To Eliot, Lucas, Ben and Sam...*

*You inspire us every day.*

—Jennifer & David Stone

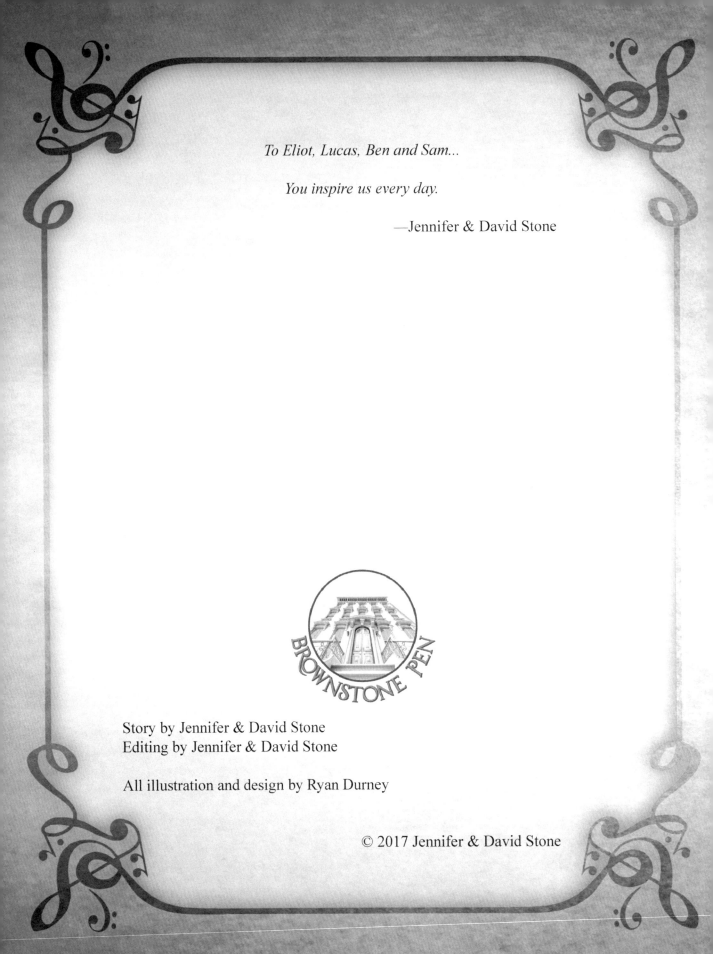

Story by Jennifer & David Stone
Editing by Jennifer & David Stone

All illustration and design by Ryan Durney

# Mirabel and the Magical Music Shop

by Jennifer & David Stone

*illustrated by Ryan Durney*

Mirabel lived with her little dog Claude in a snow globe in Lincoln Center.

Lincoln Center is a magical place where people go to see the symphony, the ballet and the opera.

The Center was especially magical at Christmas time when snow was on the ground and the square was filled with children.

Next to Mirabel sat statues of famous music composers Beethoven and Mozart. Below Mirabel was a shelf with bow ties, glass ballerinas and toy soldiers.

Mirabel's dog Claude wasn't your typical dog. Instead of biscuits, he loved buttery croissants. During the day, Mirabel was lonely because she had no one to talk to except Claude and the only thing he ever said, was "Arf."

But at night, Mirabel was happy because the shop-keeper Jenny would sing to her while she polished Mirabel's snow globe. Then Jenny would lock the shop with a big golden key and the real fun would begin.

This was a very special shop because one December night, many years ago, a Magician who was appearing in the famous ballet, "The Nutcracker," had entered the shop and sprinkled magical stardust all over the gifts. From that night forward, every night from midnight to daylight, all of the gifts came to life.

Bow-Jangles, the bow tie, would dance a jig; the glass ballerinas would pirouette and the soldiers would march around drumming and shooting their pop guns.

Elsewhere, Mozart and Beethoven would argue about who was the greatest music composer of all time.

Mirabel did not even know what a music composer was. She had never heard music. The snow in her globe was always blowing loudly. The only thing Mirabel could hear well was Mozart snoring. He snored so loud, that every gift in the shop would wake up until the fairies got him back to sleep.

Tonight, the gifts were all buzzing with excitement.

Mirabel asked Beethoven, "Why is everyone so excited?"

"The Magician always comes on Christmas Eve," said Beethoven.

"That's right," said Mozart, "And each year he makes one gift real for one day."

"I hope he picks me," said one of the soldiers. "I would love to fight in a real battle."

"No, me!" said Bow-Jangles. "I'm going to dance on Broadway."

Mirabel desperately wanted to be real for a day. She wanted to feel real snow on her face not soap flakes.

Mirabel wanted to hear music and dance among the moon and the stars at the fountain in Lincoln Center.

Finally, Christmas Eve came. All of the gifts were so excited. Who would the Magician pick?

Suddenly, a man in a black cape appeared in a cloud of smoke. He had eyes like sparkling green jewels.

"He'll never pick me," thought Mirabel. "There are so many gifts and I am so small."

But before she knew it, the Magician stood at her globe. "Hello, pretty little girl!" he said. "Why do you look so sad?"

"Because I want to feel real snow and hear real music," thought Mirabel.

The Magician seemed to hear her thoughts. He said, "If I make you real, will you obey these three important rules?

"One, stay away from the Opera Cat.

"Two, don't go in the Opera Hall.

"Three, return to your globe by midnight. If you don't, you and your dog will turn into snowflakes and blow away."

"I will," said Mirabel.

"Very well then," said the Magician and waved his black wand.

Suddenly, Mirabel began floating like a cloud through the glass of the snow globe.

"I can't believe it–I am a real girl!" Mirabel exclaimed, "And I am going to hear music!"

The Magician waved again and Mirabel found herself and Claude standing in the middle of Lincoln Center.

She felt real snow for the first time! Claude and Mirabel twirled in the snow and looked up at the beautiful stars!

Suddenly, Claude ran off. "Oh no, Claude thinks the moon is a big croissant!" thought Mirabel.

Just then, Mirabel ran headlong into a man with long coattails walking briskly and carrying a black stick.

"Are you a Magician?" asked Mirabel, looking at his stick.

"Certainly not–I am a musician," he said. "I am Alexi Kropotkin, the famous conductor, and this is my baton. Don't you recognize me?"

Mirabel shook her head.

"Run back to your parents. Little girls don't belong here," he said, striding off.

"But I don't have any parents," Mirabel thought to herself.

Then she saw Claude's little tail wagging behind the fountain.

When Mirabel got to the fountain, Claude was not there. Instead, she saw a large gray cat dressed in a tuxedo with a little black top hat.

"Have you seen my dog?" she asked.

"I don't have time for seeing dogs–I am the Opera Cat," said the cat.

Mirabel noticed no one was looking at the cat even though a cat wearing a tux and top hat is not something you see every day.

"Do people see you?" she asked.

"People see me all the time," said Opera Cat, but they are too busy to notice me.

"Actually, the other cats are jealous of me because when the Magician let me leave the gift shop, he gave me these clothes and I am the only cat they let into the opera."

Mirabel said, "I'll be your friend…I've lost my dog– can you help me?"

"That depends," said Opera Cat. "Do you have any cheese?"

"I thought mice ate cheese?!" said Mirabel.

"That is a terrible misconception," said Opera Cat. "Many cats appreciate good cheese."

"What's a misconception?" said Mirabel.

"A mistake," said Opera Cat. "Now, if you have no cheese, I really must be going."

"I don't have cheese," said Mirabel, "but I have this sugar cookie."

"Normally, I don't help find dogs for cookies," said the Opera Cat, eyeing the cookie suspiciously, "But, in your case I will make an exception."

"If you know a thing someone likes, it can help you find them," said the Opera Cat.

"Claude loves croissants!" said Mirabel.

"I have an idea," said the Opera Cat, scratching his chin. "Follow me. They sell croissants at the Opera."

Mirabel thought of the Magician's rules. "Oh, no," she thought. "This is the bad cat and he is taking me to the opera and I'm about to break two rules."

Mirabel decided it was okay to break the rules. She had to find Claude!

The Opera Cat took Mirabel up a winding staircase where two small chairs sat atop one of the opera boxes.

The orchestra began to play and there were colorful characters on the stage singing and dancing. Mirabel loved the sound. It was so magical. She was drifting along  on a little musical cloud.

When intermission came, the Opera Cat said, "Let's go to the orchestra pit and look for Claude because sometimes musicians eat croissants."

Mirabel was afraid. The only pits she knew were messy peach, plums, cherries and olive pits.

But luckily, the pit was not filled with messy fruits. Instead, it was filled with people with musical instruments; horns, brass, woodwinds and strings.

The conductor spotted Mirabel and the Opera Cat. His silver hair stuck straight up and he flung his baton at them. They fell into the tuba, which let out a loud sound and they were flung into the air again!

Mirabel landed on the head of a woman holding a long wand. Only this wand had white hairs and the hairs made music. It was the most wonderful thing that Mirabel had ever seen.

"Hello," said the woman.

"What is that magical thing you are playing?" asked Mirabel.

"This is a violin and I am a violinist," said the woman.

"What brings you to the opera?" asked the violinist.

Mirabel said, "I got my wish to leave the shop for a day. I live in a snow globe and I can't hear music."

"This violin is a Stradivarius," said the woman. "It is very old and expensive. We are playing "The Magic Flute" by Mozart.

"Tomorrow night we are playing "Beethoven's 9th Symphony." He wrote it back in 1869. Did you know that Beethoven was almost completely deaf when he wrote his symphony but somehow he still heard the music in his head? Here, let me show you."

Mirabel wondered if the violinist knew about Mozart's snoring. She giggled to herself.

As the woman played, Mirabel loved listening to the beautiful music but then she remembered Claude. "I'm sorry. We must go and I have to find my dog."

"Let's follow the conductor!" said Opera Cat. "He likes croissants!"

As they were leaving, the violinist took out a tiny violin just Mirabel's size.

"Please take it with you. Keep it as a gift from me," said the violinist.

"Remember, the real music is within you, so you can never lose it."

Mirabel and Opera Cat hid in the conductor's coat-tails so he couldn't see them.

The conductor sat down in his dressing room and unwrapped a big puffy croissant.

Suddenly, Claude's head appeared from the conductor's coat pocket and snatched the croissant.

"Give me back my croissant, you mutt!" yelled the conductor, shaking his baton at Claude.

Before he could react, Mirabel grabbed Claude, and ran out of the back door clutching Claude in one hand and her violin in the other. Suddenly, Mirabel's hands felt funny. Mirabel looked at the clock.

"Oh no! My hands are turning into snowflakes!" Mirabel thought. "It's almost midnight!"

Mirabel rushed into the music shop just as the big grandfather clock was striking midnight. She looked up, and saw the Magician frowning and looking at his pocket watch.

"I'm so sorry I broke the rules. But I had to find Claude," Mirabel said. "Please, Mr. Magician, I don't want to be a snowflake!"

The Magician smiled. "Mirabel, you are a sweet girl. I see you learned many important lessons on your adventure, not like that Opera Cat who disobeyed me last year."

He waved his wand and Mirabel's hands turned back into real hands. She felt herself floating back into the globe.

"See you next year, everyone," said the Magician, and he vanished in a puff of smoke.

Mirabel was happy to be home with her only real family. That night, she told all of the gifts, "I learned a lot on my adventure but most importantly, I found the music within me, and the music is love."

The next morning when Jenny the Shopkeeper was dusting the gifts, she noticed Mirabel didn't look as sad.

Then she noticed something else. Mirabel was holding something new. "I don't remember that being there," said Jenny.

Mirabel smiled and winked.

# About the Authors:

When they are not writing children's books, producing films or writing, producing and directing plays, Jennifer and David Stone live in Berkeley Heights, New Jersey with their sons Eliot and Lucas, their dog Watson and their pet fish Sherlock.

# About the Illustrator:

Ryan Durney is a full-time illustrator in Austin. He has a BFA in illustration and has garnered several awards, such as a *Children's Choice Award* and recently a *Preferred Choice Award* by Creative Child Magazine for the story book *Princess Willow & the Magic Fairy Brush.*

In his limited free time, he writes short fiction and illustrates it, as he's done in his series *Birds of Lore.*

*www.ryandurney.com*

Made in the USA
Lexington, KY
15 March 2018